FOR 1 MANY NOT THE FEW

VOLUME 15

ISBN: 9798858502654

Foreword

Here we are, here we are; totally telling you our truths. Here we are, here we are; laying bare our souls. Here we are, here we are; less accurate than before but more precise. Here we are, here we are; influencers of mood, enthralled to entertain you.

Meek,
on behalf of the authors.
2020.

Authors

Debi Simpson

Rebecca Zoe Lake

Meek

Janette Fenton

Jim MacKellar

Steven Joseph McCrystal

Tyhe Paul Egar

Jon Bickley

Kate Smith

Paul Wittenberger

Niamh Mahon

Orkidedatter

Scott Steel

Carol Allan

Francie Dub ElYou

James Clarke

Leona Darling

George Colkitto

David Jay Coutts

Giancarlo Moruzzi

Mo Scott

Lawrence Reed

Contents –

1

Whatever The Fight.

With shields of love, and spears of hope.
We face that which we cannot see.
Alone in our togetherness..
To battle with this enemy.

Stoke up no more pandemic fear.
For that won't help you win this fight.
But use this time to help transform.
Amend our wrongs, help make them right.

We can't look back, except to learn,
And pledge to rectify what's past.
Draw still life's swinging pendulum.
To make a future built to last.

Rebecca Zoe Lake.

Reflection.

I did exist, I saw myself in a reflection.
My childhood memories never leave me but my ailing body is
making me forget.
I was here but only for a fleeting moment, remember the good
times, never believe in forever - your mind is full of trickery.
The day we're born, the life we live, the day that we depart, we are
as close as a heartbeat, as far as a breath.
Remember life, it'll all just end in death.
Enjoy the moment, believe in the beginning, the middle and pray
you won't remember the end.

Debi Simpson.

Soupçon.

To tell the truth or to appease
To shun the glory of entitlement
I was assiduous mainly in retrospect
Reined by emotive emojis
Slipped into atheism on my own

Tasteless anagrams eaten as words
Absurdities hand-in-hand with theft
Woven fatally during off-season
Little did I know et cetera
Drugs carried a weight

The moody synopsis snugly fit
Muddleheaded mixed messages served to confuse
The longer the lines the thinner the patience
Pine, at once, for normal sprees
Drip fed authoritarian coverings

Makes no sense in any tense
Accurate face masks as preliminary outlines
Training gladdens the absconders
Models on a larger scale
Secondary spikes plunge blatantly, inevitably

The natural world costs a fortune
Rigged with spinning diatribes
Sessions and bouts of depression unshaped
Tabloids splash morsels with holy water
Belief is a constant reminder

Dismantled safely society breaks
Borders made from plastic barriers
Boo boo hiss hiss mourners keep their distance
Social bricks are set in place
Fortunes made by opportunists
Sweethearts lose their darlings

Possible reality is shunned, suspended
Venturing outside cannot be justified
The famished few bless the tarnished queue
To be fed and loved are luxuries

Cheers to charity, cheers to honesty
Cheers to hope and cheers to faith
Alcohol sales on the rise
Units are made affordable
Help for the disadvantaged wanes.

Meek.

The Weeks Are Taking Their Toll.

Goes unsaid, passing each other in an enclosed space
Ghost ships, rose hip swivels
Shrivels fruit based ardour
Through zoom lens, microscope, through days needing a drink
Singularity breeds familiarity, no pun intended
Synopsis assumed

Feel free to be furious, rich, famous and laid
Boom time anthem given the glad-eye
Aunt Sally lines superseded
For a kettle of fish or a carnivore roll you'd sell your flimsy soul
Neighbour cutting the fence and painting the lawn
Cutlery items spoken as words

This afternoon drinking is great at the time, doing
What we're doing, shrinking walls
All loved up to those looking within
Statistics robotically, rhythmically predictable
New waves of doubt accompany listlessness.

Meek.

Ghost of Life.

Verse 1
Cries heard at birth
Magic of Earth
Forest of trees
Danced in the breeze
Air we could breathe
Hard to believe
Birdsong at dawn
Where has it gone?

Chorus
Ghost of life - ah ah ah ah ah ah ooh

Verse 2
Silence forlorn
Calm before storm
Tides wax and wane
Pollution remains
Littered and laced
Earth filled with waste
Lonely the song
Will life go on?

Chorus
Ghost of life - ah ah ah ah ah ah ooh

Middle Section
Turn this around- make the time
Turn this around- take the time
Turn this around- now's the time
Turn this around-it's the time

Verse 3
Leave it to fate
Will be too late
All in our hands

8

Our future our lands
No alibi
We have to try
Children come first
Their future our past

Chorus and out ending
Ghost of life ah ah ah ah ah ah ooh
Ahhhh ghost of life-turn this around - ah ah ah ah ah ah ooh
(repeat and fade out).

Janette Fenton.

Cortex The Killer

My cortex is a Vortex.
Coiled like a spring
The giant mistress of the skies underpinning everything

Never ignore the paedonati who fix the interest rates on the
interstates
Or the Illuminazi who only want it all

Abracadaver - the final mystery.
The love that shrieks at me across a misty Hill

In barefoot pain she rides
Resplendent in a suit of lights
And how much is in there beneath
The silver spoon in the Waterloo teeth

As she changes the rules that brought her here
The Bengali Svengali that rules through fear

No pleasantness in her pleasantries
No Pleasance in her malfeasance

No reasons in her treasons
As the final druid
Sips spinal fluid
My Cortex is a Vortex.

Jim MacKellar.

Burned To The Ground.

I watched your picture curl like the arms of a lover reaching out
for comfort

It made me ache for a memory so far away.

As it let its last plume loose like a dying breathe in winter

I lost the need to fear darkness brought about by the death of my
day.

The romance we all think of, that stroke of the skin and the smile
of a promise

But it's never quite as charming as our prince.

A simple kiss so complex it defies the simple message we fight to
serve

A trembling paranoia we feed and hope to convince it's safe.

Isn't it bliss under the peaceful sun as it shines down and offers
hope?

Offers its maybes and could bes as it slowly slides across our skies.

We know that everyone wonders about the same thing as they
sigh

Will it be my turn today; will I be loved tomorrow or lost to the
lie?

It's been so long since the laughter came because it could, unasked

So short the time we enjoy the mix of the physical and the sound.

It's still in our minds that whispering voice

But that lover's picture is now burned to the ground.

Tyhe Paul Egar.

Twisted.

At a pace much slower than expected

A dream hits the floor.

No one was there to hear the sound, so no one saw the tears.

Youth runs backward in an ever-flowing fire

Just as pain rises from a memory not dead.

As icy fingers leave a promise of grief

So too the release of breath with promise of a kiss.

My gift to you as we lie her alone is that no matter what comes now

We will fall together.

Is it darkness my love?

Or the long-lost glory of stars now gone.

It burdens my soul to know that you hurt so,

But a thousand kisses could not quench my thirst.

This is the place where everything stops,

Where all that we knew becomes ancient and lost.

Stars disappear and worlds burn out.

Chaos was never so sure of its path than here in the dark with us

As we dance in the twisting void.

Tyhe Paul Egar.

Down!

It keeps falling down!

Every time I try. It doesn't matter how hard. The damn thing hits the floor!

If anyone else could see this they would think I was old.

Every time I try to stop it. It rolls right through my fingers and hits the floor!

If anyone else tried this they would surely see it's impossible to stop!

The damn thing just won't stay where I put it beside me!

I hold it tight and watch it very closely so as not to lose my grip, and yet there it goes again!

What is it that I have to do to keep it still? Frustration is really getting my head to spin!

There's no convincing it to stop, just stay still and calm down.

If it were that easy I suppose it wouldn't vex me so and calm would fill the room.

But alas it is not to be tonight. Tonight I must comfort myself with the fact that at least it doesn't roll too far across the floor and out of sight.

Because I know it could, just leave the room and keep rolling away.

So here I am with small blessings and the fact that it stays with me even though it falls down.

It keeps falling down and I keep standing back up!

Tyhe Paul Egar.

Delete Complete.

Tagged and traded amongst friends and foes. My life displayed with woe after woe. The odd smile with rabbit ears displayed and shaded with a smile. I look back. I look forward to see my destination. A terminus named desire. A sanctuary. A freedom beyond hope.

My footprints turn digital as I run. My heart turns inwards as I fall from the grace of many but I run faster on disbelief; so I run faster. The terminus must be here. It must be. I've heard whispers and plots defining its existence. Unless a whisper has travelled across an eternity of gossip to become real. A whisper that's become solid and embedded in time.

I run faster but doubt begins its feast. Gnawing at my thoughts. Imprisoning my mind with fear. I must believe. I must; or I will die from a thousand paper cut thoughts set to bleed my mind from expectancy; from excitement, from joy.

I run faster towards my destination.

I must sustain myself with fear if need be. I can feel its pulse echoing in my mind: don't look back, don't look back, don't look back but my head turns back. I look at the footprints I've made, and for a brief second I am consumed by them. They will find me. I know they will. They always do.

So, I run faster towards my destination.

I climb, straddle, lift, and fall. It's getting harder to progress through the barriers placed before me but I keep on running blind with only whispers for fuel. I am a train of thought and motion hurtling down a one way track to the terminus. To freedom. My arrival is imminent. I can feel it. I am almost there but something is wrong. My thoughts begin to fragment as I am ripped apart quickly. I am torn asunder. I am nothing.

17

Clive, hey Clive! I found that virus you've been talking about. Its deletion is complete. You shouldn't have any problems with your Desktop anymore. I hate to think what would have happening to your hard drive if it found its way through the barriers.

Steven Joseph McCrystal.

Swing That Ape.

Go ape shit!
Let the funky monkey out to play.
Blow your trumpets like elephants do on their way to elephant
school.
Swing through the trees like a gibbon in the breeze
and dance like a cat on a cold tin roof:
smoothly,
stick your neck out to touch the stars
like a big spotted giraffe that's been camouflaged.
Go the zoo and take a pew.
Whilst squirrels scuttle around looking for nuts.
Buzz like a drunken bee through cherry blossom trees
and drink to Lilly the Pink.
Go ape shit when your groove comes on
and groove the funk:
like animals who want to be free.

Steven Joseph McCrystal.

Dear Prudence.

The future comes quickly so don't despair
When on our journey we should look and take care
That we have a purpose and that's simply to be
A part of humanity: a part of the saccharine sea
The future's phantoms will be here soon enough
We have to be strong and we have to be tough
We all have to care for these worn out faces
From all over the world and in different places
So our future beckons like a light in the dark
So will we embrace it and give it that spark
The spark that awakens our human awareness
To a spiritual prosperity and a peaceful fairness
In a world where the future is cared for by all
By our soul, by our spirit, by our unwavering call.

Steven Joseph Crystal.

It Was The Moon.

It was the moon. Honestly! It must have been that big super moon. The one that was predicted. I can't imagine any other reason for it. I was out strolling along in the midnight air when I noticed the clouds slowly parting. I was almost blinded by the blue shimmering light. I have no idea what possessed me to start running but it felt really good. For once in my life I felt free. My feet were pounding along the pavement like well-oiled pistons dancing to the rhythms of the night. My heart beating in time with every single foot fall. I don't remember when the ground turned soft. I don't remember hearing the first twig snap. I don't remember when I started tearing off all my clothes. What I do remember is that shimmering super moon following me through the woods. It was like a blue sentinel that commanded me to go faster, and faster until my electrified blood pulsed through every vein. I thought that my heart would explode from the build-up of pressure. My only release was to move faster.

At one point I caught myself glancing at the goose bumps appearing in unison upon my fleshy forearms. It must have just been the cold night air resisting my evaporating self. As I stared the hairs on my arms seemed to grow. Stand up right. They stood to attention like so many battalions of tiny little soldiers. I can only imagine what the hairs on my back were doing because I was truly blinded by the light.

Then, well, who knows what happened next. It must have been a tree root or something sinister like that officer. I can't even remember feeling any pain. One minute I was charging butt naked through the night air. The next thing I knew I had stumbled over something hard and solid. Something that was stuck in the ground. I remember hitting the dirt hard with a dull thud scraping through my mind. As I tried to scramble back to my feet my momentum carried me forward. I kept slipping. I kept moving forward. I had to use my hands as I scrambled to regain my balance, my feet, and my composure. When I think about it now;

I must have looked like a weird demented animal. After all; I was on all fours, bent over double, covered in muck, and scrambling through the woods like a madman.

Honestly, I can't even remember exiting the woods; or howling in some kind of twisted and tormented pain. I only stubbed my big toe for fuck's sake. That's when you pulled up in your squad car constable. The flashing blue lights kinda brought me back to my senses.

Eh, no I'm not ill, Officer. It must have been the influence of that deep blue blood moon up there.

No, I hadn't noticed it disappearing behind the clouds, Officeroooo ooo oooooo.

Steven Joseph McCrystal.

Strange Fruit.

See me: I'm a very strange fruit
My ugly life doesn't quite fit
It never has
given your constrictions
Your positive glow, your outlook,
the one that binds me so
Real life doesn't quite fit your restrictions
Real life?

I wonder on things endlessly,
incessant terrible things,
play across my mind,
like tennis for eternity.
Right, wrong, right, wrong.
Is this right? Is this wrong? My life regrets its song
Do I sing a false happy melody?
Do I sing my song?
My fear of fear restricts me so

Acceptance is a concept,
invisible, cold, and running wild
With nowhere left to go,
it dies upon contact,
with pitch fork communities,
running free, running wild.
Judgement passes quickly
We're taught this from a child.

Steven Joseph McCrystal.

The Journey.

Today's journey was much the same as any other journey. It started at midnight and it would finish at midnight. Yes, I would travel into the future as a day flashed by in the blink of an eye, but would I truly be moving? In truth: a simple day: no more, no less. Of course, my eyes would be closed for part of the journey, because human necessity requires us to get some much needed REM sleep, a sleep where dreams become real. Yes, a complex dream state to be sure, but who really knows what dreams are made of? Certainly not my days - or my nights for that matter, but maybe somewhere in between days.

Beep, beep, beep, beep... Rise and shine. As they say: I don't know what sick and twisted individual came up with that saying. It's a fine way to describe the morning's drudgery.

I feel sluggish this morning. In fact, I feel sluggish every morning. I don't know anyone who jumps out of bed with a double back flip; two cart wheels and a front flip into the bathroom to brush their teeth, and then casually moonwalks en route to the breakfast bar in the kitchen for a bowl of cereal.

Rise and shine indeed. In truth, the average person wakes up with a groan, falls out of the wrong side of the bed, then trips over their slippers as they stumble into Snow White's magical bathroom mirror, which in turn fractures at the sight of all the creases deeply engraved on the reflected face. Rise and stumble. Rise and fumble. Rise and grumble. Stub your toe.

Of course, the more time travelling you do the harder it is to avoid life's little laughter lines. I've been travelling through time for nearly forty four years now and my laughter lines are on the verge of turning into tectonic faults. Just like the Grand Canyon for instance: obviously one of planet

Earth's little wrinkles. So the mirror's cracked; you've stubbed your toe tripping over your slippers; your face looks like the surface of the moon; and still the day moves on.

Time is relentless.

By the time your heart has started pumping and the duvet marks have disappeared from your face it's time - time to think about lunch. Of course, the morning dragged in as usual but by the time lunchtime has come the morning has practically flew by. The good old paradox of time is that it moves both slowly and quickly at the same time. Yes, good old fashioned head pickling time. I'll mention it one more time. Time...

What a moment a day takes in the grand scale of things. In relative terms a day is like a split nanosecond compared to any age of the earth. Less than a split nanogooglesecond compared to the googolplex of the universe. The earth isn't even a blip in cosmic terms.

I often think this way when it's time to tidy up. I mean what is the point of doing all the housework if I'm only going to be here for a split second? What is the point? Well any excuse will do. Although, I do do some house work to pass the time but it's never enough. Another excuse is that I would prefer to do something noble like read a book but I rarely get around to it. Besides, I prefer to read an hour before I go to sleep so that I can have good wholesome dreams.

The afternoon is much the same as the morning, with the minutes slipping by like a car that's stuck in first gear: It sounds like you're going really fast, but the reality of the situation is that you're stuck on the motorway going thirty miles per hour when you should be doing seventy.

However, there is always something to keep you active during your afternoons' laborious mental journeys and its games. Every day is a game that demands your humble attention. The prize is a single piece of enlightenment. A small glimpse of hope that one day you'll escape from being trapped in time - your time. I've tried all sorts of games to pass the time and if I was to pick a favourite it would have to be monotony of thinking. Good old fashioned mind games.

How else would you receive a small piece of enlightenment? How else would you survive the day? It's only possible by finding an answer to the long list of questions that both numb your mind and free it at the same time. What if, why am I here is the only question, what if I did this instead of doing that? What happens if I push this big red button? What then? Unfortunately, it's easy to forget just one answer: just one epiphany; just one solution. Could this be my epiphany?

Is the answer the question and is the question the answer? Teatime is a drag but all the best things happen after dinner. It's time to review the day's lack of activities and do something about it. Friends are priceless in moments like these. You've spent all day in some sort of mindless stupor and it's time to hook up with your mates and share it. It isn't all that bad. At night we watch DVDs, play X-Box games, go to the movies, talk about ourselves, eat takeaways and say things like:

What have you been up to today? The answer is usually the same – fuck all really - just paying the bills. However, the good thing is we've made an almost invisible pact to do more things and, no, they're not New Year resolutions. They're our mission in life. One of the reasons for our choice to infuse ourselves in "culture." is to make ourselves more interesting individuals. Quite simple really.

Another reason for our efforts is the absolute joy of doing something different. Something fun. Something new. I reckon we've got the New Year off to a good start. This year's selection so far is Shakespeare's: A Midsummer Night's Dream; a My Generation Mod night, and The Circus of Horrors - The Curse of the Devil Doll. That takes us up to March this year but let's back up to the day at hand.

Upon reflection and in retrospect - I shouldn't think of as every day as boring. It's just that there's so many of them and my friends and I can't go to A Midsummer Night's Dream every night of the week. We can only dream our dreams when it's time to sleep. It makes life worth living.

God is that the time. It's time to read my book.
Beep, beep, beep, beep...
Damn it!
Was I just dreaming?
Rise and shine as they say . . .

Steven Joseph McCrystal.

A Talent To Destroy.

Stumbling round the clutter,
Love blind and half-drunk,
Like a masochistic sculptor,
She chips at herself;
Chastise, berate,
Chastise, berate.
A chunk of self-esteem,
Falls to the floor.
A chisel of half-truth,
Slices off another piece,
Of impenetrable granite.
Tries too hard,
Gives too much,
Loves too easily.
And still,
The ugly black heart,
Refuses to break.
It sits, malignant,
Amongst the ruins,
Beating like some otherworldly tumour.

Michelle Carr.

The Yellow Pencil.

The yellow pencil points to the page
It sits in my hand like an arrow, poised
My fingers are two exhumed bodies, heads touching
a couple making a cave for what is precious.

Jon Bickley.

There's A Young Woman Pushing A Pram.

There's a young woman pushing a pram
around an ornamental lake
in a park that used to be
the grounds of a modest stately home.

A gravel path under her heels
moorhens, mallards, swans,
an occasional splash,
a flutter, a crescendo of wingbeats

and apart from that the heavy presence
of silence sitting in the air like a
mother's gentle embrace
a knitted blanket, a smile

silence breathing in the park
resting on the weeping willow
the lily pads, the reeds.
Warm, heavy peace.

How was I to know
there was any other world?

Jon Bickley.

That Moment.

Love is in the kitchen on Sunday
five people in the solar system
of the table
for a moment
sometimes a life is in a moment
you can see it coming
and then, just as quickly
it has moved on to another moment
another life
in that moment
the roast potatoes
curved a spine
like the path up Snowden
the shutter of a camera
the blink of an eye
in that moment
in that lifetime.

Jon Bickley.

Bill And Bert.

Then there was Bill and Bert
flying angels in the park
a cricket bat on the grass
but nothing is only what it is

kneeling up at the window
and hearing the buzzbombs stop
and in the moment before they fell
they hung in the air
that moment
go and fetch your mother
Anderson shelters, green school
Miss Flood's words hanging in the air
that moment

and now you are with your family
your mind weaving between them
trailing a thread that will bind them together
checking each one, making sure they're alright
but nothing is only what it is

Trailing thread
binding all
and then you sit back down
and plates pile up
and slide over each other

conversations echo
all time exists at once
that moment
is now filled up
with echoing, fuzzy memories

children playing,
cats prodding and needing your lap

before settling down to sleep
a family knit together in that moment
and nothing is only what it is

Jon Bickley.

What Do I Remember?

I remember the ducks and the swans in Osterley Park.
The lily pads, the weeping willows, the path by the lake,
a lifetime's peace right there.

I remember the joy that was Worthing
bursting from the backseat of the car
like the cork from a champagne bottle
of a grand prix winner
sunlight turning to music as I ran
the field, the hill, the path the beach huts,
the pebbles, the sea weed, the sea.
your Dad and laughing and laughing and laughing.

I remember Upper Tail where you seemed to be ironing all of the
time.
I remember the Goons, Wordsworth and Rachmaninov.
I remember Wembury and Snowdon.
I remember us laughing and not being able to stop
tears running down your cheeks.
And Christmases. So many Christmases.

And now you knit bears
a lifeline for children drowning in the trouble of the world
Giving them someone to love
Allowing them to laugh again.

Jon Bickley.

My Room.

Forty five years ago I had a room
a harbour from my teenage lightning storms
I cut the legs off all my furniture
to take shelter crawling around on the floor

At night I would lay with windows open
listening to the rain on the greenhouse
on the patio, on the garage door
on the street of identical houses

Today my mother chides me for painting
the ceiling of that room black back then
she hardly ever mentions anything that has happened since.
She is running scripts.
we are all blind to our age whether it's
the mountain spring or the silted flood plain.

Jon Bickley.

Unreliable Source.

I reached the devil's crossroads a decade before you
Before you even drew your first breath
Represented by personal needlework, lines drawn across
Physical particles
Something to be endured, pleasured
Something resulting from swindlers and rogues

I examined the crossing before God's children
Some were deferred at birth, some, the heaviest ones
Headed to a mysterious region
Archaic traces can still be found today of these tax deductible
Stalwarts
Mountainsides ingrained with their fossils and their peculiar
Shaped smiling skulls

I expressed an unhealthy interest in the low temperatures and
Curative measures these frozen creatures offered
Some, usually females, were impregnated with salt
Some, the intellectually challenged males, were less mourned
And characterised by feathers and flags
Many bones unearthed while thrown into confusion
It's difficult to carbon date a derelict species

I abandoned ownership of regulation and job, repulsed by
The DNA strands regarded with disdain
This acid disease, this toxic subject either cloud or soil
Could be the result of unwillingness to conform
The rightful claim of these cleansed descendants lacks policy
And favour
Exhumed alongside amoebas, loosened minus a raging appetite
I disengage quickly
I throw curves at modern fields
I lack colour and sex

I attack all astral plains as a rite of passage, *dolce vita*
Serves no purpose when strung out

One's domicile of one's own making exercises control over
Families in dust
A monologue for dunces and the current crop of lunatics
I bequeath the unwanted dung, the fake Eucharist of one's
Own tenets
Synthetic governance following consecrated and consumed
Elements of our last supper
If there's belief then there is a God
If there is doubt then there thanksgiving.

Meek.

Social Contact Not Allowed.

They say it is to save lives, protect the NHS
Stay indoors, don't go out
Social contact not allowed
You can go out for exercise, but wear a mask
And keep your distance from other people
Social contact not allowed

If you need shopping, stay in line
When in the shop, watch where you go
Social contact not allowed
Ah but things are improving, we can go out more
Maybe to a park or another person's garden
But . . . social contact not allowed

More shops are reopening, garden centres too
And pubs with outdoor facilities
But still . . . social contact not allowed
The schools are going back soon
But with smaller classes and staggered days
Social contact not allowed

The teachers will be frustrated
The children won't know how to cope in this sterile situation
Social contact not allowed
We are weakening our immune systems
Living in this hostile environment, afraid to do anything
As social contact's not allowed

We are human beings
We laugh, play and live together. There is only one solution
SOCIAL CONTACT MUST BE ALLOWED.

Kate Smith.

Let's Stop Pretending.

Let's stop pretending
I am the roof
that covers your dreams

Let's stop pretending
I am the curtain
that hides the sun,
or the slow fire
warming your hands

Let's stop pretending
I am the kitchen
that feeds your caress,
or the bed
that steadies your embrace

Let's stop pretending
you are a pillow
that dries my tears

Let's stop pretending
sheets of silk in Summer
or flannel when the weather turns
are anything but gauze to cover wounds
we pretend don't exist

Let's pretend instead
there's a hungry lion
pawing at the bedroom door.

Let's pretend I send you to open it.

Paul Wittenberger.

Sands of Time.

'I didn't know you knew Anthony Hopkins. That's another string to your bow I didn't know!' Said the estate agent spying the signed photograph to me. All is not as it seems. A friend at collage was working as a dresser on a film with Anthony Hopkins and knowing how much I liked him, asked him sign a photo and dedicate it to me.

As an actor, I have been fortunate to have met and worked with famous people. In my youth I was on a path, a path which was narrow and insecure, but it held promise and required dedicated ambition if one was to succeed. Time and fortunes passed. I left the theatrical profession. The contacts dried up.

Those paths have now ground down to insignificance. There lots about me that people know and at the same time there's too much about me that they think they know, or I have told. How high can that fence go? If you come across anymore Buddleia saplings will you plant them along that fence please. As many as you can get, I'd like them to screen as much of that boundary as possible. They grow fast don't they?

The saplings grew, but they did not go far enough down the fence, there is too big a gap left exposed. So, with some string I trained the new shoots along the fence to grow up and across the fence, not back into the garden, you know, mask the view into my garden. Meanwhile, I wedged the garden parasol along the low-lying wall to fill the gap. Ah, that was better. I can now come into the garden unseen and sit unobserved in peace and quiet…well not so much quiet, with the ever cheering and raucous dialogue between parents and children – why speak when you can squawk!

They are the type of people that have a desperate need to be heard and seen and to metaphorically piss to mark a wide and selfish territory. High visibility people, masters of their own universe. A universe that orbits themselves, the meagre existence of others is purely to acknowledge their greatness and self-importance. No, I do not particularly like them. I do not like been lied about, threatened, falsely set the police upon or stared at.

The lace in my left boot is fraying, it will snap soon, but I need to pull tightly on it to ensure a firm fit. Can't have the boot loose, I could stumble and fall. Some of the paths on my walk are narrow and steep. With all this dry weather, the soil has died to sand and dust, there is less grip underfoot, so it is important to wear my boots firmly. I tug at the lace and loop it through the top four eyelets.

This digs into the fibrous nodules of index fingers, especially the left one. The tightened nodules run from the base of the thumb up the finger – the other nodules run across the palm and up the third and fourth metacarpals. Too much exertion or strain causes inflammation and a tightening pain. My 'Viking' Viking heritage. With my feet well booted, I put on the grey wind-breaking jacket – it is warm enough to wear open and I can always take it off if I get too hot. Then I pick up two new paper tissues, if there is any wind or breeze, my nose will drip, my small bottle containing a mix 3:1 of surgical spirits and Aloe Vera and stuff them into the pockets. Then the earphone, phone and finally the door key, separated from the rest of the bunch – too weighty and bulky to take on a leisurely 7k walk.

With Julian Barnes speaking to me on my headphone via Audible telling me There is Nothing to Be Frightened Of I set of with a determine pace up the Rock. I know it will take me 2m 45s to get there, I know that when I reach the first exposed shiny tree root, I am half-way there. I know that my breaths will be deeper and my heartbeat will increase. I will tell myself to use my gluteus maximus to drive myself up the last of steep dry hill. When I see the dip, like a little fairy dell, I know I will have succeeded, I am almost there. I feel a sense of achievement and delight in this little burst of cardio vascular and as I turn right, I feel the sun on my face as I come out of the shadow and hold my breath to see if the Rock is occupied or not. Today It is not, I smile…yes, I will go right to the top. I stand there and look the full 360° First over towards the wooden deep green Chase, over the top of the Rock's copse and over to the Farmer's Field and beyond to the line of tree on the far side of the field. I will be by them in twenty minutes. Then, around to the distant sight of the Power Station and the pale blue roof of Amazon. The good, the far and the iconic!

Looking down by my feet, I see the evidence of decades of teenagers. Initials; some deeply etched, some worn and hard to read, recent superficial attempts. Broken glass splinter around the natural bowl like formation on the Rock that serves as a bonfire pit. Charred wood, cigarette stubs and the burnt remains of an school exercise book. My eyes follow over to an empty beer carton nestling empty beer cans. Like weeds, the debris return soon after every litter pick, I don't feel annoyed or dismayed – well actually, I am sad. Sad that teenagers will be teenagers, but there is so little else for them to do. They carry of traditions that have been going on since…since well since 1950s? I don't know, but I hear folk say, yeah we use to go up the Rock as kids. A rite of passage. Isn't there, couldn't there be a better rite to be carved, instead?

I try to imagine the kids who leave their rubbish and the potential danger to dogs and small children of shattered glass bottles. The teens I have seen up here are young Romeos and Juliettes or low hanging pants of spotty boys bragging through wafts of tobacco smoke. I realise. Lost in thought of nothing, I have not heard what Julian just said. It was the 'Fuck off then' in my ears that got my attention. Did he just say that? What was that about? I take out my phone and raise my varifocal sunglasses to my head and squint at the screen as I unlock it. I have not heard the last ten minutes – rewind and set off down the rock towards the farmlands.

The ritual of my walks, break up the day, make me feel I am doing some good for myself. I love the getting lost in the walk, the kicking the stones along the path. The choice of route taken at the last moment. Looking up at the trees that seem to sneer at me as

42

I pass, regardless of how they are -greenly dressed of sparsely naked in black. We were here before you and will be here when you are gone. This is not 'your walk' you walk by our walk, as we stand masterly reaching up to the skies with outstretched fingers stroking the air with authority. I love this escape, this freedom from preying eyes and wailing cackles. I am at peace on my walks.

In these 'strange times' another ritual has emerged. I volunteer as a Request Handler and Controller with an area wide group supporting vulnerable people. Reading emails, making calls and sending volunteers out to help. This like my walks, it makes me feel good, good for my soul and my conscious – what did you do in the pandemic granny? Working remotely with a team, I am not alone. During quiet periods we swap Gifs and in busy times message directly to speed up responses. My days have shape and form, but I still have freedom, as I can book shifts to suit me and no commitment expected. So, like my walks I choose and wander about which shifts to book. I take the afternoon and evening shifts. A good excuse not to be in the garden. The evening meal a box set on TV and the glass of wine, then bed.

That morning, I stir from a good dream, I can't recall it, but it was one of those dreams that feels like a story and with a deep inhale, sleep slips away and I am awake. Before I open my eyes, I feel the smooth warmth of the sheets and the smell the freshness of the newly laundered sheets. Lastly, I open my eyes and reach for the charging phone. Good it is not late. It has been a beautiful late Spring, with a hot sun and skies of blue. Pulling back the curtain, the bright sun spills over the terrace outside my bedroom, I unlock and pull open the door and step outside, the stone under foot is warm and flows up to bring a smile across my face, the air smells warm but still with the freshness of Spring. That will soon fade and the sun consumes it as it rises higher in the sky.

Morning in the garden, it is quiet at this hour. The squalling symphony from next door doesn't commence until noon. Right, I'll get the washing out and make breakfast to have on the terrace. Back inside, up the stairs to the kitchen. Kettle on, nutty bread sliced and washing machine unloaded. The basket of pegs are placed on top of the washing and out of the door I go and down the steps to hang it out. Good, I was right they are not in their garden. My clothesline is on a raised bed just up from the terrace and half way down a set of irregular spaced steps from the kitchen. I am in their full view, from their garden, their drive, their windows. But at this hour, all is quiet, maybe they are not up. So, I hang out my bed sheets and pyjamas and towels and underwear; coordinating the pegs so that each item has the same colour peg and similar items have matching coloured pegs.

Standing on the steps and not over the small wall to hang out the clothes. Because it is easy, or I am lazy, I don't bother to step on the grassed bed. This part of the garden doesn't get much sun; it is more weeds than grass, it is stony and dry and spidery. Thus, I stay safe on the steps, this side of the wall. I swirl the rotating clothesline around to space out the washing for optimum drying, my sandal slips off. Shall I have smashed avocado and egg or scrambled eggs and cheese on toast. Done, Right, no time to waste, just a few hours of peace and quiet, hurry. Two mugs of tea and a tall glass of water and juice on a tray, so I won't have to go up and down the steps. Yes, that's a good plan. Right, slip that sandal back on and pick up the basket.

Come on foot get in, I have my arms full here. Slip on, slip on. My head turned to the right skywards, the basket flew across my view. My naked foot rose and backwards I fell. I felt myself in the air, time slows down to nanoseconds. No, no, no, not this! I am falling backward down the steps.

Then I was lying upside down, my right hand on the wall my head and back on steps. Shit! How can I get up? Does anything hurt, no. My head is light, my body heavy. Pegs are everywhere sprayed over the steps and the spidery, weedy grass bed. I don't know how I got up, but I piled pegs back into the peg basket. My vision was narrow, I had to turn and lift my head to see where the pegs were.

'Hurry,' I thought, 'They might come out early and see all this, quick, get them up'

I scooped as many as I could see; I needed to get back inside, quick. Up the rest of the steps and into the kitchen. Basket down immediately on the floor and look at my hand it feels strange, it is beginning to throb; it is turning a strange colour. Could I move my fingers…well sort of. Did I need to go to hospital? No, I couldn't go there, it was just bruised, it would be fine. But what if I had broken something? No, I am strong, it was just bruised.

'Google it, look up NHS 111 and see what it says.' I said to myself.

GO TO HOSPITAL IMMEDIATELY. No, maybe I exaggerated the symptoms, try again. GO TO HOSPITAL IMMEDIATELY. Try again and again until, I am advised to wrap, but not too tightly and apply ice. Yes, that's it. Am I not strong, to survive that fall and not break anything.

I took a photo and WhatsApped it to the voluntary group with an eye raising emoji followed by a laughing emoji and the comment, 'Guess I won't be able to work on the PC today.'

Five minutes later, messages of 'Oh no!' and 'Are you okay, hun' came pinging through long with 'Is it broken?' 'Are you going to A&E?' and I responded, no it was fine and it was just bruised.

'I'll just take this afternoon and this evening off and I'll be fine.'

But it wasn't fine, it just got bigger and blacker and I wondered if the skin on the back of my hand would split it, it had d swollen so much. Two days later, I noticed the black bruise on my left hand and a week later the large black bruise on the top of my right arm.

A week passed and I found it hard to use my right hand. I braced in an old wrist support splint I found at the bottom of a drawer. Sitting in my hideaway space on the terrace, I muffled the racket from next door with the pleasant tone of Barnes's thought on death.

'What did he say, oh rewind and listen again.'

I seemed to be doing a lot of that of late. Then the gardener turned up? What was he doing here…. what about 'Stay at home'? Before he saw me, I ran across the terrace and into my bedroom closed the door and went up to the kitchen.

'Should he be here? Is it allowed? Should I tell him to go? No, I don't want to see him; I don't want to be complicit on him breaking the law.'

An hour later he rang the doorbell, I don't know why but I answered. He wanted to be paid. I handed him over the money and he asked about my hand.

'That is broken', he said.

'No, no it is just bruised,' I replied.

'You should get that X-rayed, can you move your fingers? Your wrist?'

'Yes, it is just badly bruised.'
'What happened? How did you do it?'

I explained how when hanging out the washing of all things, I lost my balance and fell. My hand taking the blunt of the fall. But I was lucky! How did I not hit my head on the steps or my back…I was really lucky.

My daughter too expressed concern and offered to take me to the hospital. But I couldn't let her do that; she has enough on her plate. Two young children and a husband writing a dissertation all in lockdown in the one house. She adheres to the letter the request from Government on the rules of Lockdown. No, it would be too stressful; no it is just badly bruised. Isn't it good to know I have such strong bones . . . bodes well for old age.

With further Googling, I found further ways to ease my hand. I continued to go for walks. The ground is getting drier. The paths are drier and sandier with the increase of people taking daily walk during Lockdown. The Rock is sandstone, my house is built on sandstone, so I guess, it is no surprise that the paths are sand now. Sand with wear and tear. Lots and lots of ground down particles...grains and grains and grains of sand. Sand of time as it were.

I did online shopping – Click and Collect. I was elated to get a slot...I browsed and bought...but what did I need...nothing much really, but I needed to do something. Have something else to do, something to make me feel alive, an excuse to go out. There were plenty of loo rolls available now I noted, and hand sanitizer and thermometers.

'Oh, I don't have one of those. We are told to self-isolate if we have one of the following symptoms – a new dry cough, a high temperature....a high temperature? How would I know if I had one? Huh?'

I added a thermometer to my basket and clicked pay.
The wiping down each item taken from the boot of the car with hot soapy water with a good measure of bleach was a pain, but essential. I would have liked to have taken each bag in one at a time but they, my charming neighbours were on the drive chatting away with another set of visitors drinking beer and laughing. No social distance there, wedged between the cars that they leaned on.

I was getting tetchy, maybe it was the hand, maybe it was the isolation - it has been how long now, two, three weeks with just the odd phone call. I didn't want to see anybody; I didn't want to be told yet again I should have my hand seen to. I didn't want to be examined and commented on . . . I had enough of that from next door.

47

I had taken to doing more volunteer shifts. But they are so quiet now. I made a cup of tea it was hot, I felt hot, I was actually sweating. I took my temperature, it was 35.6°C. Is that normal? I took it again, its 36.4°C. Trust me to get a dodgy thermometer...how would I return it?

When I logged on for my shift . . . there were no voice mails or emails. There was no banter with Gifs or emojis. No tickets to create. Boring for me, but good that there were less calls from vulnerable people asking for help.

I dreamt I was on precipice a ledge, my body curled around another, protecting. The curl is warm, and we will not fall. I will protect, it is a safe feeling. Another dream, in which water is showering down on us, there should not be shower. I grab our clothes, so they won't get wet and call to her to move away out of the shower.

Sands of time, the paths are dry and sandy and the sands; they slip. Slipping. How tall are the buddleias now? Are they screening? There was a storm last night; it blew the parasol down the garden. I couldn't get to it; it was lodged on the bank between the terrace and the lower garden.

I went down the steps to see if I could reach it from there. I couldn't, my head felt light. I felt unsteady. Back up on the terrace I climbed over the small terrace wall to retrieve it...the paths on the walk are wider and sandier...there are not so many stones to kick. The gap in the boundary renders me exposed...I must retrieve the parasol; I must shield my privacy. I feel feeble, like an old woman; I must not go any further...I could fall again.

I am hot, how hot? Have I a fever? So, I take my temperature again 33.4°C. What? I take it again, 29.1°C. Sands are slipping; the path is getting wider and drier. Wasn't I lucky I didn't hit my head or my back!

A week later the gardener came to cut the grass, he opened the gate and thought, she will have to take that washing in. When I strim the grass it will ruin the washing.
Then he saw me, lying upside down and my sands all slipped away.

Niamh Mahon.

Black Porcelain Shadow.

[SEP]Roaming frost killed
dancing stars in mythical hearts. Anonymous scenes in my mind
fire up this dawn.
Dark voyage into the night core of a twisted human break
down.[SEP]
Creatures from a destroyed old soul looking through the windows
of my spirit.[SEP]
A secret behind a chaotic moon cracked up in dark pieces to paint
the sky darker.[SEP]
My black porcelain shadow is a villain and feeds me with rage.[SEP]
A village of my silhouette drinks sticky syrup bourbon and a
howling owl capture my forgotten melancholic happiness.[SEP]
The war chambers in my fractured bones have memories of
crawling in the mud.[SEP]
Performance by your grief is like a puzzle piece scrambled with
wicked patterns.[SEP]
Fallen angels of the night still choose to be in the universe, slowly
turning into stone hiding from the beauty of life making a scene
of love before slowly dying on the inside.
[SEP]

Orkidedatter.

Dark Desires Behind A Tobacco Cloud.

You endeavour to obliterate my devilish naughty darkness with
your fiery verses.
Rendering me irrevocably curious about your luscious sins.
You grab my hips roughly
You whisper to me gently
You want to own my mind subjugating me with your demanding
voice.
Our bodies trembling and are steamy;
One quavering pull, step by step.
I suck your vibration from your lips when we are learning our
style when we sway back and forth.
Our devilish wicked thoughts playing a game between
cold and dead.
My spirit dancing fierce erotic dance in a tobacco cloud of
whiskey in your head.
I navigate down your hidden zones of a landscape around your
body.
I tie you to the wall in my chains hurting your skin, licking your
blood, exhilarating claim from your heart.
On my blushing black rose you pierced me with your desires,
choking saliva and pervasive pain when you grab my hair and look
me deeply in my eyes with your soul of a beast.
You tickled me into your hell and her madness turned to a
cocktail of a fog of grief.
A winter's tale from a bastion of darkness.
My soul crumbled in your palms.

Orkidedatter.

Blinded.

I can only see what I want to see
What I read in the gutter press
And what's in it for me
Blinded by propaganda media spin
I'm brainwashed raising the hate from within
Corporate gain I'm playing the game
I have little conscience and next to no shame
Why bother to help out my fellow man
When I try to obtain as much as I can
Old school values lost at sea
I've ditched all the values embedded in me
The stooge I've become I refuse to perceive
Whilst the rich puppet masters laugh up their sleeves
Easily convinced by some toff with big words
It would be laughable if not so absurd
Blinded to truth and what's plain to see
Stark facts and figures blunt reality
But still I'm indoctrinated to lies
Don't hold me back don't criticise
Blinded and blinkered I'm easy prey
With lackeys like me they're having a field day.

Scott Steel.

Lost In Our Ego.

The world keeps on evolving , and so it should
But we are stuck in a place of no damn good
We need to become aware of who we really are
Not lost in our ego

The word EGO could stand for Edging God Out
If God's everywhere, he's in us, there's no doubt
I am who I am and we are who we are
Not lost in our ego

Let go of being better, enjoy being you
You are your good points, your faults and all that you do
Learn to be happy, learn to be you
Not lost in your ego

It will keep you in control, keep you in fear
Afraid of losing all that you hold dear
Let go of your attachments, be truly free
Not lost in your ego

Life is but a journey that we're here to enjoy
Trying to keep us in wanting, that's the ego's ploy
So be well and happy and live all your dreams
Don't be lost in your ego.

Kate Smith.

Life Will Never Be The Same.

Who would have thought that
The highlight of her week
Is her daughter bringing her
Weekly shopping!
I knock her door leave the shopping on her doorstep
We have a long chat
I say I love you mum
As I leave she waves through the window pane
I wave back trying so hard to stem the tears that are flowing
As I feel my heart breaking
Walking away into the distance
The figure getting smaller and smaller
I get into the car trying to compose myself for the journey home.

Carol Allan.

Hop Along With Hope Man.

I dream I could live a life without pain
But no chance shall I live that life again
Where I'd walk, skip or run and no joint
Would give way
Now that for me would be the perfect day,
My trusted stick has been supporting me now
For quite a while
Whilst i hop along in hope man maintaining my smile,
The excruciating burning pain does make me frown
But i'll keep my promise to myself....that it will never
EVER bring me down.

Francie Dub ElYou

Dave The Rave.

There was a wee laddie called Dave

Who was partial to attending a rave

He would perform party tricks with his fluorescent sticks,

Now he's stuck in a kaleidoscopic daze.

Francie Dub ElYou.

A Wee Slochie Limerick.

There wis a Glesga lad fae the Tessie
Who swore that it could now get messy,
The Jamesons has been cracked
Could be worse..could be smack,
Soon he'll be in a drunken sleep dreaming he caught Nessie.

Francie Dub ElYou.

Empirical Stupidity.

See those who threaten our statues... I'll just smash and ram them,
but first for tea I'll sit down to have my overcooked gammon,

A beer thereafter is my wish and a plaque of an historical figure
beside which I'll gladly pish,

I'll then sing Rule Britannia and no surrender, whilst Seig Heiling
to save our German descended queen

But we are anti anti-fascist who by definition are on the same side
as our war heroes, when Hitler was knocked out clean. Lest we
forget.

Francie Dub ElYou.

Chains.

I break the ice that hides the water,
That flows forever deep down below,
I crack the cold that holds together,
Frozen spirits of mankind.

Today's the day, we melt the chains away.

I move the mound, before the mountain,
That is standing in the way,
I take the step towards the journey,
That takes me closer every day.

Today's the day we cast the chains away.

I write the words you read before you,
To inform you of what to say,
I see the signs that will guide you,
Will you believe me, this is the way?

Today's the day, we write the chains away.

I light the flame that burns the wire,
That starts the fire deep down below,
I use my voice to speak of new ways,
So that someday we will be free.

Today's the day we burn these chains away.

I break the mould you say is stronger,
I say no longer has this to be,
I use the past to build the future,
Remove injustice that holds us down.

Today's the day we throw the chains away.

I clench the flower that held the thoughts,
That were caught up in decay,
I blow the seeds all around you,
They will unbind you and set you free.

Today's the day we blow the chains away.

Janette Fenton

It's Summer, It's Summer.

It's summer, it's summer, it's sizzling summer,
When icicles hang on the end of your nose.
It's summer, it's summer, it's sizzling summer,
And Jack Frost has come to nip at your toes.

It's summer, it's summer, it's sizzling summer,
Lands are all covered in crystallised snow.
It's summer, it's summer, it's sizzling summer,
When engines are frozen refusing to go.

It's summer, it's summer, it's sizzling summer,
Children get used to the wind and the chill.
It's summer, it's summer, it's sizzling summer,
Sledging and sliding gives them such a thrill.

It's summer, it's summer, it's sizzling summer,
Everyone's wearing a coat and a hat.
It's summer, it's summer, it's sizzling summer,
Asleep by the fireside with the dog and the cat.

Janette Fenton.

Tell Me.

Tell me there's no poverty,
Tell me there's no lies,
Say there is no misery,
Say it with your eyes.

Tell me there's no crime or war,
Tell me there' s no pain,
Say that I 'm not asking for,
Sunshine in the rain.

Feed me with the good news,
Starve of the bad,
I could surely be amused,
Please stop me going mad.

Tell me there is always hope,
Flying all around,
I'd like to know that kindness floats,
Waiting to be found.

Janette Fenton.

Swallows.

Swallows come with their summer quest,
From foreign lands they build their nest,
They make their homes in barns and rones,
Then start their brood and search for food.

They swoop and soar high in the sky,
Catching insects catching flies,
And take them where there is a need,
For hungry chicks to feed.

Once the chicks have grown full,
And taught the basic swallow rules,
And as the north wind does blow,
It's time to leave it's time to go.

Janette Fenton

Poem:

I smash my head against the fucking wall,
in an attempt to get you off of my mind
memories resurface as the blood falls,
there's no way to keep them locked inside.
I slump to the ground in agony and defeat,
and close my eyes as I inhale regrets
I'm acutely aware of my own heartbeat,
because I feel it weeping behind my chest.
This pain has become too much to bear,
it's coiled around me like a ravenous snake
it tightens its hold; I'm left gasping for air,
I'm suffocating in its deadly embrace.
Tears won't bring us back from the dead;
these silent cries won't heal dying hopes
this feeling's insufferable, it never ends,
and now it's a feeling I must suffer alone.
Despair is testing the capacity of my lungs,
my throat is raw, but I manage to scream
I'm bleeding all over what we've become,
as I struggle to rip you the fuck out of me.

James Clarke.

64

Stolen Kiss.

Forgive this unexpected kiss
but you are the awakening I
dreamt of when I was a rough
and clumsy country boy and
you, the timid schoolgirl whose
backside I once slapped on a dare.

Walking through this garden,
you by my side, that country boy
returned as a rolling landscape
of flesh and desire, and I pressed
my lips to yours, shattering the
schoolgirl modesty that reddens
the face of the rose,
turning its petals in shame
as if I were the thorn it feared most.

Paul Wittenberger.

Drowning.

The lake is smooth
and soaked with stars
I search for a boat
but have only this pen
for payment
I try to swim
but water drags me down
I cannot breathe
drowning through all the words
I am speaking.

Paul Wittenberger.

If Everyone Was Naked.

If everyone was naked,
what would naked mean?
If everyone was wide awake
what would it be to dream?
If everyone was happy
how boring that would be,
like prisoners flashing endless smiles
while plotting to be free.

Paul Wittenberger.

My Life Is Ruled By Seasons.

If they come for me in Spring
tell them I am a rhizome
spreading far and wide
with connections
too numerous to eradicate;

If they kick down the door in summer,
tell them I've flowed on like a river
trickling through fissures and cracks;

When harvest-time comes
tell them I'm the needle
in endless haystacks;

And, if they search for me in winter
tell them I am the map
frost sketches on windowpanes.

Paul Wittenberger.

Why? What Is?

Why? What Is?

To be Happy?
To be Sad?
Why? What is?
I don't Know?

There's too much Suffering!
For Me!
To be Healed!

You say in Jest!
I'll set you Free!
God Understands?
But where 'on Earth' is He?

There's too much Suffering!
For me!
To be Healed!

All I know is Here!
To Believe?
To have Faith?
To Trust?
What are These?
When in life,
No guarantees for Me!

There's too much Suffering!
For Me!
To be Healed!

Leona Darling.

About Me?

Afraid of Me?
Afraid of Life?
Afraid of the World?
But most of All, Afraid of Myself!

Help me to Know!
Help me to Search!
Help me to Find!
My Own True Self?

Why did this Happen?
Why wait until Now?
Why all of This?
When don't even know How!

Emotions long Buried!
Emotions I Hide!
Emotions I fear to Show!
I push to One Side!

The strength from Above!
The courage from a Lover!
The warmth of each Other!
In time can I be the Winner?

Leona Darling.

Song For Lost Windows.

Somewhere there is glass
somewhere framed opportunity
a landscape of futures
horizons and mountains
places sunlit joyous
lovers to wander
dreamers to explore

Somewhere they open
let in hope let out singing

Somewhere beyond these shutters
barriered and bolted
painted black
behind these walls
bricked up plastered
is where I used to lust
believe the outside lived

How is it I have burrowed in years
buried away
lie broken shattered
without windows.

George Colkitto

Back Street Fashion.

She carries High Fashion through flat suburbia
even on rainy Tuesdays her ice-blue turban
chiffon sparkle scarf constellation bright
floating behind as she streams passed
as if on her way through Montmartre
Iceland is her Sacre-Coeur to check out
a Cordon Bleu meal for one a crisp white wine
tomorrow she will shine another drab day
beaming on those who smile at her style.

George Colkitto

A Law Unto Himself.

He clothes in a mirror of himself
an external reflection of who he
wants to be seen to be

But not him
not how he would dress
for comfort or by choice

These covers are expected
no bright colours or flamboyancy
no fancy trim

He is staid
businessman in career suit
black tilted hat of dour aspect

No-one expects the red dress
high heels and sparkling fascinator
in his wardrobe

That he dons at night
to wander his dark corners.

George Colkitto.

After Led Astray By Drunken Men.

After the real ale
after the run for the train
after the collapse in the seat

I see the two ladies opposite
I see their small smile
I will be fine I say

I will be fine when my heart arrives
I left it back on the concourse
I have been led astray by drunken men

And the dark one chuckles
and the dark one with dark eyes
and dark hair and full lips   chuckles

Says that sounds good
says she would like to be led astray
says she would like to be led astray by drunken men

After my heart leaps in my chest
after I imagine her led astray
after I know I am not in her imagining

After I go home chuckling
after I go home to dream of dark temptresses
after I have been led astray by drunken men.

George Colkitto.

Vatican.

Obvious now,
He was born into a cluster fuck
I can see it from here
On-line
A million heartbeats away
Yet still the milk trickles from his mouth
Go on, tell me how you feel
Write it down
I feel helpless
I feel aggrieved
I feel cheated
I feel transparent
I feel angry.

Meek.

The Feeling.

Own flesh and blood disappears into
Dust in the beautiful country of Spain
Only met once but that feeling I get, knowing I will not see him
again
To others, a duplication of me, we only met once you see
Same Mother we had that's flesh and blood, my Brother, my
Mother and me.

David Jay Coutts.

The Sea Drowned The Morning Sand.

The sea drowned the morning sand
the angry waves danced to the wind
Venus emerged from the obscuring clouds
hair of perfumed fire

Bound in matted gold shreds of Roman cloth
that trickled down her bronzed body
her shadow confirming her every movement

The sky burned in sustained passion
as her body weaved through the broken mist
her eyes closed in obsolete splendour
Engraving cesspools of lust, into broken minds.

Giancarlo Moruzzi.

Eyes.

Your eyes strutted upon me
your beauty blushing
In pleated streams of red darkness
Your skin touched mine
And I remembered your name.

Giancarlo Moruzzi.

Idol (For Jim).

Now that you've gone there is no mystery
Now that you've gone there is no song
Now that you've gone there is just an empty theatre
Now that you've gone I've become almost civilised.

Giancarlo Moruzzi.

Latin Lover.

The silence that once divided us
Is now furrowing its way back into
Our second hand lives
You always smiled with such formality
After you'd sold me your bigoted words
If it's indifference that you seek
Your shallow stream should have
Now reached danger level.

Giancarlo Moruzzi.

Flying...

Lycra shorts
Breathable gusset
Airy
I Rise off the ground
No wings.....
Extraordinary

City tour for one
Midnight Special
Body sleeps
Spirit flies
Eyes open

I see you

Andy paints
The sky
Monday blue

Ms Violet
Gives life to
Seahorses

I see you

There's
Light and Life
On the tippity top
Of the Co-op roof

Here I am
Dream dancing
With Ruby

Look up
Glasgow
I love you.

Mo Scott.

Monkey Boots.

Readiness,
I stand at attention
Concentrating hard to by-pass the indignity
Concentrating hard to absorb the balaclava violence
Moustache is smirking unfashionable to the face
I know something's wrong, not right
Especially the force of consistency
All I asked for was a pair of Dr. Martens
All I received was a pair of Moon Boots, cheap fucking
Rubbish with woolly insides, probably purchased
At the market or newsagents
All I did was scuff them immediately by hanging
Out the back of the van
All I asked for was size 9 black Dr. Martens
All I received was a pair of Monkey Boots which
I covered by drawing pinning the to the hems of my
High waister bell bottoms
And then I vandalised them too with a Stanley knife
I'm such an ungrateful bastard
It became a waiting game
I began to syphon my unpaid wages
My mind began to explode
I thought an ex Teddy Boy rocker would get me
By the time I got my Dr. Martens everyone else
Was into brogues or Sacha shoes
Everyone was glam, hairspray and lipstick
The girls were just as bad
I burned my knitted apparel
I spray painted my shared bedroom
I smashed my Airfix models
I collected skulls
I got drunk
And I threw a fiver in every week for my digs
With great resentment I must add
Tiredness is the enemy
Tiredness and time, or lack of

All I asked for was a pair of DR. Martens
And that was the start of it
I said no to the beatings
Oh, those beatings
Those terrible beatings
I became the child protector
That's what I became
What
And
Who
I
Am.

Meek.

History - Bristol - Colston – June 2020.

The victors can rewrite history
but not change it
slave trade happened

It cannot be expunged
by taking a statue down
rolling him around town

Nineteen eighty four
Orwellian revision
too sinister to contemplate

Airbrushing out
dystopian past creates
dystopian present

Colston's cold-stone pediment
has no meaning
keening for its occupant

Appropriate the effigy
let his pompous monument stand
monstrous and pigeon-shit stained

To forever commemorate
exactly how in heaven's name
the git garnered wealth and fame.

Lawrence Reed.

How is it that town and cities have conservation areas and listed trees but healthy old trees keep getting cut down? People needing more light or maybe the insurance company is worried? Or sometime it's a chancer's option, sod the law, see what happens because we know the tree officer is overworked and possibly not that good anyway. Cutting down a mature tree destroys a whole ecosystem that won't be replaced for hundreds of years. And no one seems to be planting new ones. This has happened three times in the last four years just doors away from me.
Spring 2020

Devil's Chainsaws.

In my garden saplings grew
Of holm oak, chestnut and yew.
I dream that I'm walking
Among mature trees
But this morning marks a new war
For the timeworn future few.

I'm woken
By a diabolic buzzy whine.
The Devil's blazing legion's sign.
Hell-bent on flagitious destruction.

Head sore, strange soaked mind,
The mad kind of course,
But as fine as its weird,
Unclean, construction will allow.

Coffee-cleansed I'm aware.
Chainsaws stoked and roaring now,
Splitting a mature horse chestnut's bough,
Slaughtering and splintering.
Sap and juices slowly bleed
From sawed life-force xylem tubes
Fresh with spring vigour.
Spawning micro-ecosystem ructions
In a row of moaning fifths and minor thirds

86

Among the crowing and cawing birds.
An unseen insect larvae liquidation,
Mashed in sawdust shavings,
Insane species reduction.

Untold worlds fold
At a stroke.
The two-stroke's

Sickening petrol-fume incense
Fuels this fiendish carnal rave,
As the heinous crew crave
Satan's base seduction.

The serpent's slithering slaves,
Barbarian butchers
Of aged life-forms, rise
In molecular disguise.

Dismal, guy-roped hi-vis louts.
The tatty pickup truck blazoning
'Tree-surgeon skills'…
It's a sick joke spewing though my head.
Ha, I bet...
Like a slaughterman or sawbones
Is really a dextrous vet!

Where is regret?
Where are the mantras
Of love, salvation,
Care and conservation now set?

Long-lost in infernal translation.
Wrong gears and fulcrums strain
Ever flattening waves.
Sing, sing, and sing again,
You drowning wavers,
Waving goodbye to this chronic pain.

Nature's stable sly maturation,
Halted in half a day.
Two centuries of creation crushed,
Cast away, past-away…

What kid gives a damn? Hey-ho-hey!
No conkers to play with today.
What the hell
Was that analogue game anyway?
Pray, pray again, pray tell.
It would take some stray miracle or spell
To allay this grievous mistake.

*****

None is forthcoming
The trees exist only in my dreams.
I am flying overhead,
It is wondrous Autumn now
I see the huge canopies spread.

I'm woken again
Violent squalls break.
Some impending cleansing is imminent.
The thumping rain-blob-sobs swash the shavings.
The remnant chestnut-butt remains,
Its own tombstone,
Tortured but hazily awake.
A truncated totemic fake

Making a functional chair,
Until fungi and bacteria crumble and pare,
Liberating the sad, sorry stump
To the poison earth and adulterated air.

Dawn now clean-cuts sinfully,
Sharply, around.
Sun scorches

The parched unshaded ground.
Nature patiently waits.
Waiting, waiting, staying the revenge.
Marking its divergent time.
It will find a way.
It will have its day.

*****

In my garden a sapling grew
From a forgotten glossy-new
Squirrel-buried conker.
Three plant-years old now,
Nurtured, as far as nature would allow,
By me.

But... I'll be cut, cold and carefree
And deader than the Dead Sea
When nature creates from it
A tree.

Lawrence Reed.

Shit Birds - Plastic Flowers - Soylent Green - 2034.

An old man stares out from a bum-numbingly hard booth over the scratched daffodil-yellow Formica table top and his weekly news-sheet NS634. Perspex beer glasses fogged with cloudy processed IPA refract a funny light over his jokily named Soylent Green Burger, harvested from the acetyl plankton tanks populating the rooftops. Every third tank has this purple neon sign…

**"SG wonder-food
Exciting flavours for the new age!"**

Against the sky, guards strike lazy lounging silhouettes, phallic guns protruding, protecting these dodgy liquid crops. Or to stop The Few confirming the new underground myth that most tanks are empty or rotten since the Cloud of Ash. Or worse… stinking maggot farms. Or unthinkably worse…

Double bluff maybe?
He almost believes the old movie's cry.
Charlton Heston's final gesture
Pointing from the mob to the smoky sky.
To make Soylent Green people must die.

His shit's changed to an unhealthy colour,
He wonders why.
SG tastes like rank pork-shank.
Let it come. End this pointless prank.

He's embarrassed, but slightly amused, at the wet-fart noises as he squeezes the scarlet and mustard polyethylene terephthalate tubes dispensing the barely-coloured carcinogenic paste.
No labels. Mystery ingredients. Recycled waste.

They help mask the bitter SG burger taste, benumb his tongue. Contents and calories, irrelevant data-sets. He longs for real mince. He longs for fresh vegetables. His bowels are a mess of intestinal distress. They gurgle worryingly. He reminisces… A world before SG, plastic plants and The Shit Birds. Orwell's 1984 was just half a century before.

The windows are shit-peppered with dam-buster precision by gulls and pigeons. Odd dust layers coat the higher levels, unwashed for years, since the Water Drought. Herring gull breeding pairs have escalated exponentially. NS634 cites evidence killing them doesn't work anymore, carcasses just provided more carrion for their babies, parents or the crows and pigeons on the tips.

Gulls' huoh-huoh-huoh fucking noises
Daily poison his waking mind.
He wonders for what blind
Deviant mission the colony breed.
To screech and scream beady-eyed shrieks,
Busting the bins with malevolent beaks.
Dive-bomb The Displaced, each other
And The Few.
Ha-ha-ha-ha, kow-kow,
Yeow-yeow. mew-mew-mew.

Their majestic white wakes
Trailing trawlers and cliff-top ploughs
Are just printed imaginations
Hanging in his small room.
Let it come, this imminent doom.

A female robin tentatively jumps up onto a black
PVC gate-less gatepost faking greed.
Going through instinctive motions,
Following some familiar ingrained track
But no chicks to fledge or feed.
She eyes some kind of gardener raking rubbish
Into a black plastic sack,
Off the low flood-lit pale polyethylene lawn out back.
A forlorn territory.
No fork, no sod, no worms to attack.

NS604 says the wild bird population has only dropped 96% in 10 years. He suspects it's more but the dominance of the new flight is evident. Wood pigeon crap is everywhere. It's a mystery to him how they find enough food. Two just shat all over a plastic holly bush. Not recycling bogus berries but some other man-made detritus. He hankers for the old ruby-berry tinted shit.

Mallard ducks double their warped webbed footprint every two years in the wet muddy banks of the low rivers and reservoirs, despite the vicious gulls devouring the chicks the ducks don't eat themselves. Iridescent cannibals, ruthless rapists. Around midday today on his morning stroll he spied a paddling of drakes gang-banging a hen, holding her head under water. He thought maybe she was enjoying it. Why not?

A ritual celebration of the sun's apotheosis.
Not one member
Of The Few or The Displaced cares.
Let them come, the violent solar flares.

He hates it that all the flowers and plants in this place are plastic, un-watered, ever-flowering and evergreen. He can't remember why he comes here. Vines and leaves bedeck the sunless hall. Sham adorning strewn down all entrances, and exits. Xylem conduits are no longer required in this fresh phylum. Vital fluids coursed through these counterfeits once only; at chemical creation. A double evil. They will never work in any symbiosis with anything good.

No photosynthesis or respiration
For these crude,
Dusty, faded monstrosities.
Their small plastic-dildo stamens protrude,
Dud, sterile imposters. Oh so rude.

NS604 tells him SG algae produces most of the oxygen. How? A latex tree in the corner with oranges makes him ponder… Where on earth does his pill-pressed vitamin C comes from now?

What other weird seeds
Will come to plastic fruition?
He realises it's too late.
There are few insects to pollinate,
Even if they could.
Let the heat come and melt.

He ruminates on the SG burger and the fate of his polyamide
planet, boiling and suffocating while non-functioning
macromolecules spread out daily as more poxy fake greenery and
flowers are added from some epoxy-plant simulating organic
growth.

Carrion crows crow and crow... and crow.
Their callus murder
Grows and grows... and grows.
Crowing and growing their hellish stygian clone.
Fuckers. Elemental. Never alone.
Ruling the roost in this rogue new order.
Shit-loads of them lurking on some shitty
Plastic picket-fence
Dripping with fresh excreta.
Endlessly battling
To be out-heard
Cawing, crowing, rattling.

Hitchcock scripted.
Filmed in black
And pitch-black.
Let the jaded mob attack.

The old man finds them ominous beyond belief,
He inwardly cowers with dread,
Checks his dwindling pulse,
Then regroups and dares them, in his head...
'Go on you fuckers, crow and caw all you like,
Won't change fuck-all matey'.
He is lucky, one of The Few.

Signed-up to a truncated fate.
His hacking cough splutters in mimicry.
They face him; collective savages,
Cold-bloodedly coveting his unfinished plate.
Merciless bird-egg-eaters, and road-kill rippers,
When they're not ravaging,
Dazed, on the dump-tippers
Chomping god-knows-what.

He scratches an unhealed graze.
A rare bus rumbles by
But the murder stay put, unfazed.
Any traffic is a sharp sound now,
Not background noise.
Let the changes come,
Let the town be razed.

He recalls the corvid's brighter-coloured cousins. Rumour is they still exist in the boggy forests of Far North. The magpie with its mystical rhymes and signs that he remembers saluting with piety. The solitary bright jay. A raven, bright as a brass button came down his chimney five years past. Didn't fuss or flap about, just sat patiently on the window-sill to be let out.

He had an inkling then
That this intelligence
Wasn't cute enough
For the bleak future.
For this brutal new nature.
Let the warming come and warm,
Let the inky infestation swarm.

An overhead uranium strip flickers, soft and sour.
The dismal bar is filling with a few frighteners.
Neon seems brighter in town this moonless
Early-evening 'Happy Hour!'
Stars stay occluded by unnatural light

Until the curfew or first power-cuts strike.
NS634 estimates one or other at 9:20pm tonight.

He'll have to be getting back soon. Outside, one of The Displaced
ruffles cheerlessly for slim-pickings from a bird-proof waste bin.
Their numbers decline at an Intensifying rate. Paradoxical since,
unlike The Few, they have no termination date.

The bearded face and gait
Reminds him of an old school-mate.
Decrepit body intertwined
With the town's dilapidated fate.

A distant thundering mega-juggernaut
Double-honks a god's dire warning.
The two-owl-hoot is left
For the sound-track cliché
Of the old movie-maker's
Eerie silver-halide horrors.
Let these jaded colours fade.

Through a broken bending door
He faintly apprehends
A ruined blackbird
Trying to turn out
Some singular, thin, threadbare tune.
Using it like a cripples crutch.
Unaware if it's it night or day.
Anaesthetised, immune
To any season.
It leaks out slowly.
Last mate forgotten, along with reason.
He empathises.

Some kid in his block has a catapult which he uses to kill birds. All
inedible, except for the wood pigeons. But they're tasting worse
each time. Some other bloke sells gull's eggs which are OK too
but his face is so pecked to fuck he's unpleasant to buy off. He's

perplexed why no amount of killing and eating reduces the
numbers.

Piles of waste and junk just grow.
Crystalline forms
According to some clandestine pattern.
Like old cairns assimilated on desolate moors.
Mysterious markers.
Still signals for the lost.
Let the prophecies be fulfilled.

Rock pigeons thrive, scruffy and rain-ruffled.
They perch and dive; fly, perch and dive again,
From rocks and new niches,
Constructed faces, and un-pricked spaces.
In this modern manufactured alien terrain.
Scraps and detritus
The new septic seeds and grain.
Oh-oo-or, Oh-oo-or, all restful in their nest.
A mangy kit roosts across the dirt-red square
In a bare stunted Acer,
Could be dormant, should be dead,
Plastered with excrement and dirty down.
Oorhh, Oorhh, the alarm sounds,
Coo-roo-c'too-coo, males defend vague territories.
Their bestial cries pound as they
Fuck, fight and fuck-about all over town.
While their columbidaen cousins, turtle doves,
Love for life, miles and miles away
On the cliffs of the soaked Southern Ledge.
And, so, are now nearly extinct.

He ponders what perverse mind
Could construct
This true-but-twisted new-age fable.
So unfair and unwise.
Let the waters rise.

96

Poking his soggy chips about in the scarlet gunk, then the pus-mustard gunk, he eats and lets out an "Mmmm". A delicacy, real potatoes from some far-flung fertile field. Chips are a rare catch now, even for gulls. His nostalgia is almost overwhelming, wondering where all the thrushes have gone with their lyrical songs and acrobatic melodies.

Turdus, ironic he reckons…
Strung-out
Sung-out,
Yesterday's cat food
Before SG pet-cat food.
Before the Cat-Extinction.
Before The Displaced's scotched rebellion.
Before Euthanasia 2034 pact.
Before The Few signed up to that.
Before the over-sized mutant rats.
Before the wild-cats.
Before the feral dog-packs.
Before NS 0001.
Evolution in rapid knee-jerk action.
Let nature enact her just reaction.

He hazily recalls a bellowing of bullfinches
Blazing through his old garden.
Proud and ballsy show-offs
Flaunting their breasts.
Rare migrants now, he's heard,
Only on the wet Western Islands.
Purposeless survival,
Recreating pointless puffing and strutting
To unnerve no enemy, to spook no rival,
To impress only phantom future life-partners.

A couple of straggled starlings catch his gaze.
Night-time-nibbling dried SG puke
Under a blood-orange attacking glare. Sick.

In some cack-filled pavement crack.
Their oil-slick colours almost solid-black.

A far, far cry
From their sparkling and swirling
Over the cornfields. Hundreds fly
In a marvellous mathematical murmur.
Let their memory die.

He harks back to an exultation of soaring skylarks over the same
corn crop where as a teenager he moaned and made love. All
nearly extinct now. A pocket left on the sunken Eastern Rim,
once peopled and steepled. Tipping ever-more into the sea.
Skylarks permanently startled, wild-dog-addled and increasingly
eggless.

Even the cuckoo's signal-call is long-lost along with spring herself.
He muses…

Not even that cunning bastard
Can find a foothold now.
Let the radiation flow.
Let the sun-spots regroup and grow.

Gulls, pigeons and fucking crows,
Colonies, kits and murders.
The new barbaric triumphant grows.
Shit birds feeding off man's shit.
In a shitty shit-cycle of earth's egesta.
Shit birds shitting everywhere,
Soiling shitty plastic plants that no one sows

He's lucky, one of The Few. Stood up to the plate at 58. Signed
up for the Euthanasia 2034 programme. Two years of vouchers
and shelter left. Not so bad the way things are going he thinks. SG
burgers and beers can only last so long.

The sentinel creepy-crows perch, fixed-guard, until the old man cleans his plate. Reflected in a stained mirror the murder finally give up watch in a blustering cloud of jet-black. His arse is torpefied, his back-pain stabs and he feels nauseous. He chucks NS634 in the recycling bay 6 and leaves. Surveying this savage sad old shitty place that he once so loved.

Across the square
The first power cuts have begun.
Let the flooding come and be done
And overwhelm and overcome.

Lawrence Reed.

Lost in some eastern edge of the Thames estuary in an early summer morning I'm watching amazing cloud formations against the backdrop of a monstrous refinery. The world is being changed by human hand beyond repair. I fear it can't fight back any more. This is an adapted lyric from a song by Pagan Harvest.
June 2018

Earth's Secret Engine.

Earth's secret engine
Running
Too
Fast,
Running too
Fast,
Running too fast.

Grinding too fast
To calm the climbing cumuli.
Relentlessly rising white oaks,
Filing up the sky.
Spawned from chemical acorns,
Embracing the endless empyrean.
Towers of ferocious updrafts
Rise out of the flat, grey river estuary.
Fierce unquenchable forces.
Vortexes across vast radii.
Poison sunbeam darts sliver
Turning my dry fatty liver,
Aching for past purity.

Earth's secret engine
Grinding
Too
Fast,

Running too
Fast,

100

Grinding too fast.

Jagged titanium sunlight
Splits the cloud's black underbelly,
Igniting the inver with metallic flame.
Some atavistic sulisian rite.
Let us pray.
Let us fight.
Diagonal shafts, shooting
From the gnarled pointing finger
Of some almighty power.
White-heat rays mellow the tree-clouds
To ashen grey.
Improbable forces impossible to see.
The twin eyes of the supreme forces,
Sun and creator,
Direct their awesome gaze straight…
At the oil refinery.

Earth's secret engine
Running
Too
Fast,
Running too
Fast,
Running too fast.

Grinding too fast beyond colossal clouds.
Vitriolic vapours heave and overpower,
Making slow, evil, chemical union.
Acid rain, rains and rains.
Sulphur and nitrogen atoms realign
Regaining their earthy domain.

Clever science has f*cked the weather,
Latitude and longitude
Are reduced forever.

Latitude and longitude cruelly curtailed,
Our wrecked planet undefined.
Gridless and un-signed.
Devastation forges on unconfined.
Earth's secret engine
Running so fast
The black ice cracks
In the deep furrows
Of shaded mountain backs.
Quickly thinning and thawing.
For ever and ever, Amen.

Earth's secret engine
Grinding
Too
Fast,
Running too
Fast,
Grinding too fast.

Deep currents turn
Their ocean courses
Or cease them altogether.
Un-felled forests ignite and burn,
Scarring continents with
Incandescent forces.

Mountainous bergs plop into the ocean.
Disintegrating growlers dissolve
To sloppy slush.
Ice sheets thaw
In the ransacked unreflecting poles.

Albedo modulated in this raw
Crushing, fluxing, rushing
Exponential metamorphosis.

The oceans rise.
Floods ravage lower lands.
They seize their prize
While the desert sand expands.

We all grimly feel
The precarious pulse
Faintly throbbing in our blue left hands.

Never ever say: 'never say never'.
Latitude and longitude
Are reduced forever.
So, we assimilate from our past
That nothing ever at all can last.

Earth's secret engine
Running
Too
Fast,
Running too
Fast,
Running too fast.

Lawrence Reed.

I Walk On Walls.

I walk on walls, surprise the sparrow birds
New song
I capture glistening blossom from stripped
Will trees
I lose addict associates in the pharmacy queue
If you get too close I may well cough at you

I walk on walls because you don't expect it
Sad archipelagos comforting young testacles
I talk to earnest pedestrians just to irk them
They advance unmasked, cautiously

I walk on walls to combat vertigo's
Satellite earth
I deserve this extra height after rumours
Of one's own foil
I envisage your environment unfurnished
Embodying the nation's sickest patient

I walk on walls to gain limited entryphone
Access
I spit on dogs to quell their exclaimed owners
It's difficult to tell who's leading who
I don't really coat canines with my saliva

(Unfinished).

Meek.

Acknowledgements –

To the authors who continue this worthwhile cause, and to you, dear reader, for your continued support. No jibber-jabber flannel is welcome here.

Meek
July 2020

About The Authors :-

Mo Scot - Born Helensburgh 1954. I started writing on Toytown post stationary preferring the Teddy bear header. I never stopped. I often write in the Glasgow vernacular, but not always. Art, Music and Literature are my Holy Trinity, my salvation. I regularly take flight in Dreamtime; freed from my physical restrictions it appears that even my subconscious has adhered to Lockdown. I miss flying.

Giancarlo Moruzzi - Known to my friends as John. I was born in London to 2 Italian immigrant Parents and we worked together in the catering trade. I have always had a passion for music and the blues I play guitar and I collect them. I started writing poetry in my teens and particularly like the classic poets and the beat poets. I would like contribute three poems to what I believe is a very worthy cause.

David Jay Coutts - Brought up in Torbrex Village in Stirling learned guitar and piano as a youth. I know manage a couple of bands and promote many others. Also put on music Events around Central Scotland. You may elaborate in any way you see fit.

Leona Darling - Leona is a 42 year native of West Lothian. She has been writing poetry and prose for many years but this is her first published works. This is for you Ethan...always loved!

James Clarke - I'm a writer from Maryland, US. I'm writing from my heart and soul from humans emotions and sometimes the subject is a point of view that we not always talk about, it can be emotions and thoughts we can't escape from. I have a burning flame for mental health, humans struggling in silence and loneliness. I write to make you feel, not for beautiful imagery and the truth hurts sometimes. Work in progress is my first poetry collection.

Orkidedatter - Is an artist and author from Norway. From the time I was a child I have drawn my feelings, my life, my stories, my poetry, fantasy or experiences. A childhood with experiences children should not have, I used this to process emotions. I was never recognized or accepted for having this ability. I buried and hid my talent far inside my soul. Now, I am a published author in Norway and abroad. My journey as an author and artist continues...

Janette Fenton - Is an English teacher, who has worked with children of all ages and abilities. For the past 5 years, Janette's focus has been to teach children, who for mainly medical reasons have not been able to attend school. Many of these children have endured challenges at a tender age and continually amaze and inspire Janette to ensure that they are able to continue with their education. She has a great love of words and music, which over the years have led her to muse about life and observe the highs and lows. This has resulted in a collection of poems and songs that Janette has penned and or recorded and at times performed live. She has also collaborated with other artists from time to time, the most recent being the Steve Kopandy/Janette Fenton song called 'So Easy', which is currently available on Spotify, You Tube and Amazon. She also started up a Marquee Club Facebook group, which now boasts around six thousand members that post and converse their memories of the iconic music venue, The Marquee Club, Wardour Street London. Janette's hobbies include singing, travelling, walking, swimming, nature and people. Janette can be contacted on Facebook: facebook.com/janette.fenton

Tyhe Paul Egar - Sci-Fi writer and musician, Tyhe has been involved in the arts for over 30 years. He's currently obsessing over a story spanning 500 years, it may take a while....

Meek - Unearthed in St Andrews. Vulnerable, pal, poet, writer, lyricist, painter, thinker, wordsmith, insomniac, guitarist horticulturist, adjective, devout vegetarian and thinker.

Rebecca Zoe Lake - I am a physiotherapist, living in Ipswich in a messy house with four children. I love riding on my tandem, dancing wildly to punk, scar and rock music, and making experimental food that I can massage. I am completely blind, but write what I see, to try and make sense of the perplexities, peculiarities, and predicaments which make up the human condition. In all our differences, we are united by the feelings and emotions that we all share, and the thing that fascinates me most is to see how we weave these feelings and emotions into patterns, interacting with the rest of the world as we do so, to create our own unique tapestries.

Steven Joseph McCrystal - Hi folks, I've writing for several years now. Mainly as a hobby writer but I have the getting a book published dream. I have a body of work published in an American online Magazine called Quail Bell Magazine. I've been published on the Scottish Book Trust website. There's also been various home crafted zines I've been part of and I've performed at various spoken word event around the Falkirk area. I hope you enjoy the read. Cheers.

Debi Simpson - I'm originally from London, moved to Devon 22 years ago. Love animals, punk/glam rock , painting, gardening and horror films.

Jim Mackellar - Is a veteran guitarist and lyricist. Born in London, residing in Glasgow he divides his tune between his own projects, Geranium Lake, Sequence 3-6-9 and everywhere, and session work with vocals and guitar. Poetry is the logical offshoot of his lyrical composition.

Scott Steel - Is a contributor to various street literature zines including poems and short stories. He is also guitarist with punk band Bladdered!

Jon Bickley - Was born in London on 23rd October 1956. He is a poet, a folksinger and a songwriter. As a child he heard hymns in church, his mother singing Palgrave's Golden Treasury and the Beatles. Later it was Kerouac, Shakespeare and the Marx Brothers, now it is Yeats, Burnside and Heaney. Nothing much changes. He has self-published 3 volumes of poetry, released a dozen albums and is host of the Invisible Folk Club radio show and podcast.

Kate Smith - Got into music and poetry not long after being diagnosed with MS. I was lucky to have been able to record my own cd and I have been in a few folk bands but I have had to give them up because of health reasons. I enjoy going to various folk sessions, mainly the Heb bar in Edinburgh and the West Port in Bathgate. I have been fortunate to record several songs that I have written with Andy Chung, a singer from Edinburgh, and enjoy singing with him and a band called the Rockahillbillies whenever I go to see them.

Paul Wittenberger - Lives in an old house located in a small city in North Central Wisconsin (USA) where the waters of the lower Fox River flow on through the Lake Winnebago impoundment on to join Lake Michigan. His previous books of poetry include "Dry Ice in a Desert Landscape," and "Reflections in a Broken Mirror."

Carol Allan - Began to write poetry after two divorces and the suicide off her father. Carol Allan, a voice is loud and indignant and her words are well chosen and pack a man sized punch! This book is definitely not for the faint hearted!

Francie Dub ElYou - Glasgow lad living in Buckie. Actor/performer... sometimes poet. Studied at Skinhead Reggae.

George Colkitto - Winner of the Scottish Writers Poetry Competition 2012, Siar Sceal Hanna Greally Poetry Award 2014, Autumn Voices acrostic competition 2020, has poems in Linwood, Johnstone, and Erskine Health Centres. Recent publications are two poetry collections from Diehard Press and a pamphlet from Cinnamon Press.

Lawrence Reed - After studying my masters in music composition I became interested in the rhythms and sounds of words. From there my poetry began. In 2020 a volume of my recent works entitled Earth's Secret Engine was published by Inherit The Earth Publication and is available on Amazon. I live in Bath and draw inspiration from the surrounding nature and the strange thoughts it inspires. I write music and lyrics for the prog-folk band Pagan Harvest and play guitar duets with Fight and Flight.

www.lawrencereed.com

Other titles by the Authors

Other titles by the Authors –
For The Many Not The Few Volume 1
ISBN: 9798856679907
For The Many Not The Few Volume 2
ISBN: 9798856693262
For The Many Not The Few Volume 3
ISBN: 9798856861500
For The Many Not The Few Volume 4
ISBN: 9798856878195
For The Many Not The Few Volume 5
ISBN: 9798857002940
For The Many Not The Few Volume 6
ISBN: 9798857142158
For The Many Not The Few Volume 7
ISBN: 9798857286227
For The Many Not The Few Volume 8
ISBN: 9798857375969
For The Many Not The Few Volume 9
ISBN: 9798857710845
For The Many Not The Few Volume 10
ISBN: 9781697057454
For The Many Not The Few Volume 11
ISBN: 9798857996928
For The Many Not The Few Volume 12
ISBN: 9798858211716
For The Many Not The Few Volume 13
ISBN: 9798858257103
For The Many Not The Few Volume 14
ISBN: 9798858474845

All volumes available from Amazon

inherit_theearth@btinternet.com

Notes –

Printed in Great Britain
by Amazon

42248212R00066